FIFE CULTURAL TRUST

FCT178729

KT-425-853

*

LS

Please return or renew this item before the latest date shown below

LADYBANK
LIBRARY

10/18

0 9 NOV 2018

→ NB 24.5.19

2 6 JUN 2019

1 6 AUG 2019

1 7 MAR 2020

Renewals can be made
by internet   www.onfife.com/fife-libraries
in person   at any library in Fife
by phone   03451 55 00 66

AT FIFE
LIBRARIES

Thank you for using your library

With special thanks to Anne Marie Ryan
For Marion and Richard Williams, who
have a special talent for kindness

ORCHARD BOOKS

First published in Great Britain in 2018 by The Watts Publishing Group

1 3 5 7 9 10 8 6 4 2

Text copyright © Hothouse Fiction, 2018
Illustrations copyright © Orchard Books, 2018

The moral rights of the author and illustrator have been asserted.

All characters and events in this publication, other than those clearly in the public domain, are fictitious and
any resemblance to real persons, living or dead, is purely coincidental.

All rights reserved.
No part of this publication may be reproduced, stored in a retrieval system, or transmitted, in any form or
by any means, without the prior permission in writing of the publisher, nor be otherwise circulated in any
form of binding or cover other than that in which it is published and without a similar condition including
this condition being imposed on the subsequent purchaser.

A CIP catalogue record for this book
is available from the British Library.

ISBN 978 1 40835 101 7

Printed and bound in Great Britain by Clays Ltd, St Ives plc

The paper and board used in this book are made from wood from responsible sources.

MIX
Paper from
responsible sources
FSC® C104740

Orchard Books
An imprint of
Hachette Children's Group
Part of The Watts Publishing Group Limited
Carmelite House
50 Victoria Embankment
London EC4Y 0DZ

An Hachette UK Company
www.hachette.co.uk
www.hachettechildrens.co.uk

Series created by Hothouse Fiction
www.hothousefiction.com

Pet Rescue

ROSIE BANKS

Wishing Star Palace

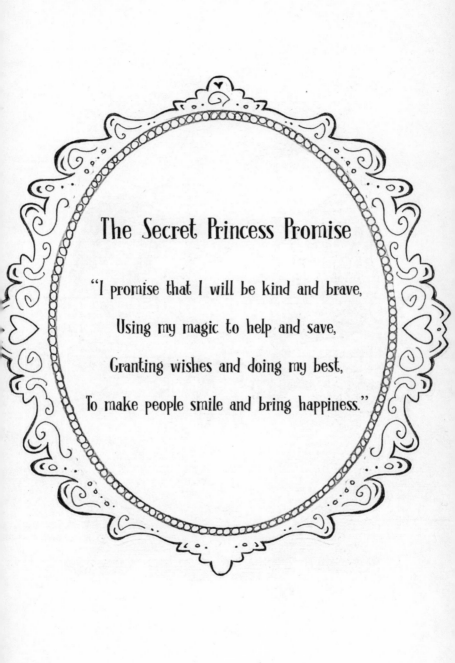

The Secret Princess Promise

"I promise that I will be kind and brave,

Using my magic to help and save,

Granting wishes and doing my best,

To make people smile and bring happiness."

CONTENTS

CHAPTER ONE
Cute Kittens

"I can't wait to eat these!" said Mia Thompson, measuring out a spoonful of baking powder and tipping it into a mixing bowl. She and her little sister, Elsie, were trying out a new chocolate brownie recipe that Mia had found online.

"What can I do?" Elsie asked.

"You can add the chocolate," said Mia.

Elsie poured a cupful of chocolate chips into the bowl and Mia stirred them into the dark brown mixture.

"It's ready to bake now," said Mia, carefully spooning the mixture into a baking tin.

The girls' mum opened the oven door and slid the baking tin inside. "How long do they need to cook for?" she asked.

Mia went over to the laptop computer on the kitchen table. She checked the recipe that was on the screen. "Thirty minutes," she told her mum.

PING! As she clicked the tab shut, Mia heard the sound of a new email arriving. It was from her best friend, Charlotte!

Clicking the email open, Mia read the message:

Hey Mia,
I thought you might like this super cute kitten video. Hope to see you soon. ;-)
Lots of love,
Charlotte
xxx

"Mum!" called Mia. "Charlotte sent me a video. Can I watch it?"

"Me too!" said Elsie, crowding around the computer screen.

"Of course," said Mum, coming over to join them.

Charlotte and her family had moved to California not long ago, so the girls often

emailed and texted each other. Mia clicked *play* on the video and an image of an adorable grey kitten with big blue eyes filled the screen. The kitten was standing in front of a mirror, swatting its reflection with its little paws.

"Oh my gosh!" cooed Mia. "It's so cute."

Mia loved all animals – but kittens were probably her favourites. They were just so sweet!

"Can we watch this one too?" Elsie asked, pointing at a link to another kitten video. It had been viewed almost five million times!

"Go on, then," said their mum, smiling.

The sisters giggled as they watched a video of three ginger kittens climbing on top of a snoring bulldog, who didn't even wake up when one of the kittens sat right on his head!

"Aww," said Mia. "Can we get a kitten, Mum?"

"Hmm," said Mum. "I'm not sure Flossie would like another cat in the house."

"Maybe we should make a video of Flossie," said Elsie.

"Maybe later," said Mum. "Right now it's time to watch Talent Quest." She pointed to the time in the corner of the computer screen.

"Yay!" squealed Elsie and Mia.

In the living room, they snuggled up on the sofa to watch their favourite television show. Flossie came and sat on Mia's lap, purring happily as Mia stroked her soft white fur.

"Tonight we have a very special guest judge," announced the show's host. "She's a former Talent Quest winner. Please welcome pop sensation Alice de Silver!"

16

"Alice!" cried Mia and Elsie together as a glamorous young woman with strawberry-blonde hair appeared on the screen. She wore a glittering gold gown and strappy high heels.

"She looks great," said Mum. "I still can't believe our neighbour became a pop star!"

"I'm so thrilled to be here tonight," Alice said, smiling into the camera. "I'm hoping to spot some exciting new talent."

Mia felt a warm glow of pride. Alice had spotted her talent already. Before Charlotte moved to America, Alice had let the girls in on an amazing secret. Alice wasn't just a famous pop star, she was also a Secret Princess – someone who could grant wishes!

Because Mia and Charlotte had such a strong talent for friendship, Alice thought that they had the potential to become Secret Princesses, just like her!

As the first contestant performed an energetic dance routine, Mum's mobile buzzed. Checking the message, she said, "It's from your dad. He'll pick you girls up at ten tomorrow morning."

"Cool," said Mia.

"Maybe Daddy will take us to the park," said Elsie.

Mia and Elsie lived with their mum, but they saw their dad every weekend and always did fun things together.

As Mum switched her phone off, Mia

thought about how the Secret Princesses
didn't need mobile phones. They had
something even cooler – magic moonstone
bracelets they used to talk to each other!
Mia and Charlotte were working towards
earning their own moonstone bracelets, but
they still needed to grant two more wishes.

Glancing down at
her magic necklace,
Mia's heart leaped.
The half-heart
pendant was
glowing!

Gently moving
Flossie on to Elsie's
lap, Mia stood up.

"Um, I think the brownies might be ready," she quickly said. No time passed while she was off on a Secret Princesses adventure, so no one would notice she was gone, but she still couldn't let her family see her disappear!

The kitchen was filled with the delicious scent of chocolate. Shutting the door

behind her, Mia held her pendant and whispered, "I wish I could be with Charlotte!"

The light shining from the pendant grew even brighter. The glow surrounded Mia, sweeping her away from the kitchen.

A moment later, she landed in a dark room. High above, stars twinkled though a glass ceiling. Mia knew she had to be at Wishing Star Palace, where the Secret Princesses met, but she didn't recognise this room.

There was just enough light for Mia to see that her clothes had transformed into her gold princess dress. Suddenly, a girl in a pink princess dress appeared in front of her.

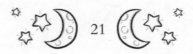

21

She wore ruby slippers, just like the ones on Mia's feet. A diamond tiara rested on her brown curls, exactly like the one on top of Mia's long blonde hair.

"Hi, Charlotte!" said Mia, giving her best friend a hug. "I loved the kitten video you sent me."

"I knew you would," said Charlotte, grinning. "When I said I hoped to see you soon, I never imagined it would be tonight!"

"I was watching Alice on Talent Quest," said Mia.

"Speaking of Alice," said Charlotte, "where are all the Secret Princesses?" She squinted in the gloom. "And where are we?"

As her eyes adjusted to the darkness, Mia's spotted a watering can, gardening tools and rows of seedlings in tiny flowerpots.

"I know!" she exclaimed. "We're in a greenhouse!"

CHAPTER TWO
Harvest Time

"You're right," said Charlotte. "I wonder why we landed here. Do you think we'll get to grant a wish?"

"There are still only two stars shining in the sky," said Mia, pointing up at the two stars visible through the glass roof. "That means nobody's wished on another tiara star yet."

The Tiara Constellation was a very
special group of stars. The four stars at the
points of the tiara were powerfully magical.
When it appeared in the sky, the Secret
Princesses granted the first wish made on
each of the four special stars. The magic
kept Wishing Star Palace hidden in the
clouds for another year.

At least, that was what was supposed to happen. But this time, the Secret Princesses' enemy, Princess Poison, had cast a terrible spell, sending a thick green mist to block out the stars. Princess Poison had once been a Secret Princess, but she'd been banished from Wishing Star Palace for using her magic to get more power. Now, she used all that power to stop the Secret Princesses from granting wishes!

"Hellllooo!" cried a friendly voice. "Anyone in here?"

The greenhouse door opened and a group of Secret Princesses came in, led by Princess Evie. The princesses were all dressed in fun dungarees and wellies. The glamorous outfit

Alice had been wearing on television had transformed into jeans and an old jumper.

"Alice!" cried Mia. "What are you doing here? You're on Talent Quest right now!"

"You're forgetting something," Alice said, putting her arm around Mia and giving her a squeeze.

"Time doesn't pass in the real world when we're at Wishing Star Palace," Charlotte reminded Mia.

"Oh, yeah!" Mia laughed.

Alice held up her wrist, showing them a beautiful bracelet with a milky white gem. "Evie called me on my moonstone bracelet during the ad break, so I popped into my dressing room and came to the palace."

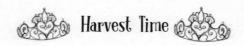

"I need everyone's help," said Princess Evie, starlight catching on her necklace's flower-shaped pendant. It showed that she had a special talent for gardening.

"Is it time to grant another wish?" Charlotte asked eagerly.

"No," said Princess Evie. "Something even more magical – it's harvest time!"

"Harvest time?" said Mia curiously. "But it's dark outside."

"You'll see," said Princess Evie mysteriously. "Now where are the baskets?" She tapped her sapphire ring and blue light streamed out of it. Evie shone the beam around the greenhouse like a torch.

"Need more light?" Charlotte asked, tapping on her own sapphire ring to make it shine. Mia did the same. The girls' sapphire rings, which they had only recently earned, flashed to warn them when danger was near, but they were also useful torches!

"The girls aren't really dressed for gardening," Princess Luna pointed out. "Could one of you change their clothes,

 30

please?" she said, holding up her wand helplessly. Luna's wand and necklace both had a moon-shaped pendant because she was training to be an astronaut. But at the moment her wand was dark green, as was her tiara. Princess Poison's horrible curse had changed their colour and blocked Luna's magic.

"Of course," said Alice, quickly waving her wand.

Glancing down, Mia saw that her princess dress had been transformed into dungarees and wellies. When she looked up again, she saw the sad expression on Luna's face.

"Don't worry, Luna," Mia said. "Someone will wish on another tiara star soon."

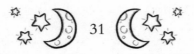

The only way to break Princess Poison's spell was to grant all four of the tiara star wishes. Mia and Charlotte had already granted two and Luna's necklace and bracelet had turned back to normal.

"I know," Luna said, giving Mia a hug. "I'm so grateful to you girls."

"Aha!" cried Princess Evie. "Found them!" She handed everyone a basket. "Anyway, you don't need magic to harvest glowberries," she told Luna.

Glowberries? thought Mia. She'd never heard of them before. She and Charlotte exchanged puzzled looks.

Evie opened the greenhouse door and stepped out into a walled garden. At first Mia thought that the bushes had been decorated with tiny fairy lights, but then she realised what the lights were – glowberries!

"It's much easier to pick glowberries at night," explained Evie, plucking a plump berry off one of the bushes.

Mia and Charlotte worked side by side, dropping ripe glowberries into their baskets. *PLIP! PLOP!* It was easy to spot the berries shining in the dark. Before long, their baskets were nearly full.

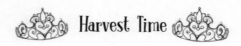

Mia popped one of the luminous berries into her mouth. Sweet and juicy, it tasted like a cross between a raspberry and a mango. "Mmm," she said. "These are incredible."

Charlotte tried one too. "It feels like my tummy is glowing!"

"Thanks for your help, everyone," Evie said when the baskets were so full of glowberries they shone like lanterns. "Let's leave a few on the bushes for the birds."

"Good idea," said Princess Ella, who loved animals as much as Mia did.

"Phew!" said Alice, wiping her forehead. "Picking berries is thirsty work."

"I've got an idea," said Princess Sylvie,

whose bright red curls were tucked up in a
bandana.

Sylvie waved her wand and suddenly they
were all holding frosty glass mugs filled with
a glowing amber liquid.

"What is it?" asked Mia.

"It's glowberry bubble tea!" said Sylvie.

"Ooh! I love bubble tea!" cried Charlotte.
"It's really popular in California."

"What's bubble tea?" Mia asked, looking
at her mug.

"Try it and see," said Sylvie, grinning
playfully. "I bet Charlotte's never had
bubble tea like this before!"

Mia took a big sip through a stripy straw.
Sweet glowberry tea filled her mouth – but

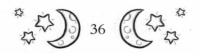

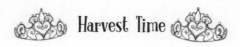

there was something round and chewy, too.

Mia bit into the chewy bubble and got an amazing blast of flavour. It was like a cross between a strawberry, a cherry and a fizzy cola sweet! "Mmm," she said. "I feel like I'm floating on air." Looking down, she saw her feet hovering above the ground. "Whoa!" she gasped. "I *am* floating!"

"Take another drink!" urged Sylvie.

Mia sipped up more tea, swallowing another chewy bubble. She felt herself rise even higher.

"Whee!" squealed Charlotte, kicking her legs in the air. "This is awesome!"

As everyone drank their bubble tea and drifted over the glowberry bushes, Mia gazed up at the sky. "Look!" she shouted, pointing at a new star shining above Wishing Star Palace. "Someone's wished on the third tiara star!"

"Yippee!" cried Charlotte. "Can we go and grant it?"

"Yes, please," said Princess Luna. "But you must be careful."

"We always are," Mia assured Luna. She floated over to Charlotte and together they drifted down to the floor. Then they clicked the heels of their magic shoes, and whirled away through the air.

The girls appeared in a round turret room at the top of one of Wishing Star Palace's towers. They ran to the huge gold telescope in the middle of the room. Charlotte quickly pointed the telescope at the third tiara star, then the girls peered through.

Mia looked through the lens and saw
a worried-looking girl with short sandy
blonde hair. She had pink hearing aids
in both of her ears and she was holding a
sausage dog with a bandaged paw.

"Poor little doggie," Mia said, stepping
aside so Charlotte could look.

"There's a message," Charlotte said,
peering through the telescope. She read it
out loud:

> "Touch the telescope to see a star,
> Call out Lizzie's name and you'll go far."

The girls gripped the telescope and
shouted, "Lizzie!"

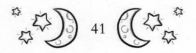

WHOOSH! Sparkling stars twinkled around Mia as the magic sent the girls hurtling through space. They were off on another adventure!

CHAPTER THREE
Lizzie's Wish

The magic set the girls down in the
countryside. Their princess outfits had
transformed back into normal clothes.
A sign reading "CLOVER HILL ANIMAL
SHELTER OPEN DAY" pointed up a
long drive.

"Do you hear that?" asked Mia.
WOOF! WOOF! WOOF!

"Lizzie was holding a dog, wasn't she?" said Charlotte.

They girls looked at each other, then followed the sound of the barking. Soon they arrived at a house with a long, low building next to it. From the noise coming from the building, Mia guessed that it was the animal shelter.

A door opened and the girl from the telescope ran out of the shelter. "Are you guys here for the Open Day?" she asked them eagerly.

"Er … yes," said Mia uncertainly. There didn't seem to be anyone else around.

"Great!" said the girl. "I'm Lizzie. My parents run the sanctuary."

 44

"I'm Charlotte, and this is Mia," said
Charlotte. "Mia loves animals."

"Then you've come to the right place,"
Lizzie said, grinning. "The Open Day
hasn't started yet, but we've got lots of fun
activities planned later on."

The girls had a look around the big white
tent that had been set up in the grounds.

There were all sorts of pet supplies for sale. There were collars and leads, chewy toys, dog beds and cat scratching posts.

"All the money goes towards running the shelter," Lizzie told them, rushing to show them one thing then another. "It costs a lot to look after all the animals."

"This is so cute!" said Mia, holding up a cat collar with a sparkly pink bow tie. "My cat would love it."

"These smell yummy," said Charlotte, sniffing a plate of biscuits.

"They're actually for dogs," Lizzie said, giggling. "They're home-made peanut butter dog biscuits."

"Delicious!" Charlotte laughed.

Mia looked at a poster pinned up to the wall. "Ooh!" she said excitedly. "There's going to be a dog show!"

"As long as enough people turn up," said Lizzie, suddenly stopping and looking worried. "We put up signs and invited everyone on our mailing list, but so far nobody but you two have arrived."

"I'm sure more people will come," Mia told Lizzie reassuringly.

"While we're waiting, do you want to see the animals?" offered Lizzie.

"Yes please!" cried Mia and Charlotte together.

A chorus of yips and yelps greeted them as they followed Lizzie inside the shelter. Inside there was a long row of kennels, each with a comfy bed and a little door leading to a big outdoor enclosure.

Peering into one of the kennels, Mia saw a brown and white beagle asleep on a cushion.

"That's Sadie," said Lizzie. "She's a big softie, but she's only quiet when she's asleep. Sometimes she barks so loudly that I turn my hearing aids off!"

The girls giggled. Then Mia spotted the
dogs in the next pen and gasped out loud.
Two golden retriever puppies were playing
with a toy. "They're so cute!" Charlotte
squealed.

"Jack and Jill are brother and sister,"
explained Lizzie. "We're hoping someone
will adopt both of them."

"It must be amazing to live around so
many animals," said Mia.

"I don't even have one pet," said
Charlotte, "because my brothers are allergic
to animal hair."

"It is pretty great," agreed Lizzie. "But
it costs a lot. That's why I really wish the
Open Day goes well – so we can raise lots of

money for the shelter. There are always lots of animals that need help. "

Mia caught Charlotte's eye and her friend nodded in reply. So that was Lizzie's wish! Now all they had to do was make sure it came true.

"Who's this little guy?" asked Mia, recognising the sausage dog with the bandaged paw from the telescope.

"That's Pickle," said Lizzie. "He's been here for ages." She opened the kennel door and Pickle limped over to her. Scooping him up in her arms, Lizzie brought Pickle over to meet the girls.

"He's adorable," said Mia, stroking Pickle's soft brown fur.

"What's wrong with his paw?" asked Charlotte.

"He needed an operation," said Lizzie. "His old owner treated him really badly."

Tears filled Mia's eyes. "How could anyone do that?" she wondered.

"I don't know," said Lizzie, shaking her head. "But we're taking good care of Pickle now. I really hope we can find him a home."

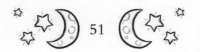

The sausage dog licked Lizzie's face. "Hey, Pickle," said Lizzie. "Want to show the girls a trick?"

Lizzie gently set Pickle down on the ground and knelt in front of him. "Shake hands," she said. Pickle offered her one of his front paws.

Mia and Charlotte clapped.

"What a clever boy!" said Mia.

"He really is," said Lizzie proudly, scratching the little dog behind the ears.

"Is Pickle going to be in the dog show?" asked Charlotte.

"No," said Lizzie. "It's for all the dogs who have been adopted from the shelter. Their owners bring them back for the show." She sighed. "We invited everyone who has adopted animals and normally lots of people come. But this year not many people have replied."

"Maybe we can get more people to come," said Charlotte.

"That would be so great," said Lizzie. "But how?"

Mia remembered the kitten videos she and Elsie had watched at home. "Maybe we could make a cute video and send it to the people on your mailing list, reminding them about the Open Day."

"Good thinking," Charlotte said. "Nobody can resist cute animals."

"Let me check with my mum," said Lizzie.

After putting Pickle back in his kennel, they found Lizzie's mum scooping dog food into feeding bowls. Lizzie quickly introduced the girls and explained Mia's plan.

"That's a great idea," said Lizzie's mum.

"Who's going to star in the video?" asked Charlotte.

"How about Jack and Jill?" said Mia. "They're really cute."

Lizzie filmed the two puppies with her mum's phone as they wrestled playfully. Their tails wagged as they squirmed around on the floor.

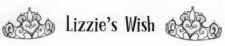

"Aww!" cooed Mia as Jill pounced on Jack and licked his face.

"Let's go and show my mum," said Lizzie.

As Lizzie's mum connected her phone to a computer to download the video, Charlotte said, "What do you get when you cross a dog with a telephone?"

"No idea," said Lizzie.

"A golden receiver!" said Charlotte.

Lizzie's mum chuckled as she watched the video of Jack and Jill playing. "Here goes!" she said, pressing send. There was a swooshing noise as the email was sent to everyone on the shelter's mailing list.

"I hope it works," said Lizzie, crossing her fingers. "We really need people to come and visit today."

It has to work, thought Mia. She couldn't bear the thought of letting dogs like Pickle down!

CHAPTER FOUR
Who Let the Dogs Out?

While they waited for the Open Day to start, Lizzie took the girls to meet the cats. Then they visited a room with rabbits and guinea pigs – there was even a pair of ferrets running in a plastic tunnel!

Finally, Lizzie took the girls into a small reptile area, where a man was filling up the water bowl in a lizard's glass tank.

"This is Ralph," Lizzie said, pointing to the lizard basking under a sunlamp.

"Don't I get an introduction?" said the man, smiling.

"And this is my dad," said Lizzie.

"That's an interesting lizard. What type is it?" Mia asked.

"It's a bearded dragon," said Lizzie's dad. "Do you want to hold it?"

Charlotte shook her head, but Mia nodded eagerly.

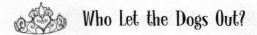

Lizzie's dad lifted out the small green lizard, which had spiny scales around its throat, and placed it in Mia's hands. She ran her finger gently along its scales, which felt much softer than they looked.

"It does feel like a dragon," Mia whispered in Charlotte's ear with a giggle. The girls would know – they had met a real dragon on their last adventure!

"It's nearly time for the Open Day to start," said Lizzie's dad as Mia handed him back the cute little lizard.

"Should we see if anyone else has arrived?" said Lizzie.

Once Mia had washed her hands, they went outside.

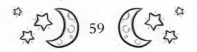

"Look at all the people!" cried Lizzie.

A crowd was gathered on the lawn by the tent. Lots of people had brought their dogs.

"I'm so glad you sent that adorable video reminder," said an older lady with fluffy grey hair. She was holding a sheepdog with equally fluffy grey hair on a lead. "I had forgotten all about the Open Day."

"Welcome back, Dusty," said Lizzie, patting the sheepdog. "Are you two entering the dog show?"

"Definitely," said the lady.

"Woof!" Dusty agreed, his tail wagging happily.

Lizzie and her parents were soon busy selling pet supplies and signing people up for the dog show.

"Are the puppies from the video still available?" asked a teenaged boy.

"They are sooooo cute," added his little sister excitedly.

"They're called Jack and Jill," said Lizzie's mum. "And, yes, they're still looking for a forever home."

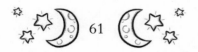

Lizzie's mum led the family who wanted to meet the puppies into the shelter, while her dad took a lady with long brown hair and glasses to see the cats. Mia and Charlotte joined Lizzie behind the display table and started serving customers.

A little boy with curly hair held up a book about dogs. "Can I get this, Mummy?" he asked his mum. She was wearing a red dress and looked very elegant.

"Don't you want a book about cats instead, Ben?" the boy's mum said, frowning.

"No," said Ben firmly. "I like dogs."

The boy's mum sighed and paid Mia for the book. As she took the money from the

lady, Mia noticed a blue light coming from her finger. Her sapphire ring was flashing!

"Charlotte!" she called.

But Charlotte didn't hear her. She was busy selling a tall, thin bald man a red tartan coat for his greyhound.

A growl made Mia jump. She turned and saw a large white poodle snarling at her across the table.

"Can I get some service?" demanded the short, tubby man holding the poodle's lead. It was Princess Poison's servant, Hex!

"Hi," Lizzie greeted Hex. "Can I help?"

"I want to see your dogs," said Hex, smirking at Mia. "Miss Fluffy wants a new doggie friend."

"Oh, she's lovely," said Lizzie, reaching out to stroke Miss Fluffy. The poodle snapped at her. Miss Fluffy was almost as mean as her nasty owner!

"I can show you the animals," said Lizzie.

"A new friend is Miss Fluffy's dearest wish," Hex said as he went off with Lizzie. Mia's heart sank. Hex was going to do something to ruin the open day!

As Lizzie led Hex and Miss Fluffy towards the outdoor run where all the rescue dogs were, the poodle snapped at Charlotte.

"Hey!" Charlotte cried, jumping back. Then, noticing Hex, she groaned. "What's he up to?"

"I don't know," said Mia. "But I'm pretty sure that he doesn't really want to adopt a new pet."

As Lizzie unlocked the enclosure's gate, Miss Fluffy tangled her lead around her legs.

"Help!" cried Lizzie as she tripped up.

The girls ran over to help Lizzie, but before they could reach her, Hex flung the gate wide open. Then he blew into a little whistle, but it didn't make a sound.

"Ha! His whistle's broken!" Charlotte said happily.

But in the enclosure, all the dogs were  barking as if they could hear something annoying.

"It's a dog whistle!" explained Mia. "Dogs can hear higher sounds than us. It's making them all cross – look!"

WOOF! WOOF! WOOF!

The dogs raced out of the enclosure. As soon as they were all loose, Hex stopped blowing the whistle and started laughing.

The dogs ran over to the tent.

Lizzie charged after the dogs. "Come back!" she cried.

"Oh no!" said Mia "We've got to help Lizzie!"

The girls ran back to the tent, trying to round up the runaway dogs. A cocker spaniel made a beeline for the dog treats.

He sprang up, resting his muddy front paws on the table.

"Down, boy!" cried Mia. She tried to grab his collar, but the dog was too fast for her.

Biting the plate of dog biscuits, he pulled it off the table. Bones and biscuits scattered all over the ground. Dogs ran over from every direction and gobbled them up the treats.

"Stop!" cried Charlotte as an enormous curly dog tussled with a tiny pug over a bone. The pug dropped the bone and the curly dog leapt back, bumping into the table of pet supplies.

CRASH! Pet toys tumbled on to the ground. Dogs pounced on the balls and

squeaky toys, their tails wagging gleefully.

"Drop!" Charlotte ordered a frisky collie chewing on a toy rugby ball.

But the collie wanted to play! He sprinted out of the tent, with the other dogs happily giving chase.

Outside, pets barked and strained on their leads while dogs from the shelter ran amok.

"Doggies!" cried the little blonde boy, clutching the book he'd bought.

"This is hopeless!" cried Mia as the curly dog barrelled past her, knocking her off her feet.

Charlotte helped her up and said something, but Mia couldn't hear it over the noise of all the barking.

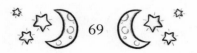

"What was that?" Mia asked.

"I said," Charlotte shouted over the din, "WE NEED TO MAKE A WISH!" The girls held their glowing pendants together, forming a perfect heart.

CHAPTER FIVE
Catastrophe

"I wish the dogs were happy and back in their pen," said Mia. There was a flash of light and suddenly the dogs were back in their enclosure.

"Oh my gosh!" said Charlotte. "Look what the magic's done!"

Now the dogs' outdoor enclosure had play equipment and a little swimming pool

shaped like a bone. There were tunnels for the dogs to crawl through, ramps for them to scamper along and even a special doggie seesaw!

"They've all been groomed," said Mia. The dogs' coats were all clean and fluffy. They even sported colourful bandanas and sparkly collars around their necks.

The tent was looking better than ever, too. There was a huge pyramid of gourmet dog bones and biscuits, and the pet toys had been arranged in a beautiful display. Visitors were shopping for pet supplies as if nothing had happened.

"Did you see that?" Lizzie asked, hurrying over to the girls.

Mia and Charlotte nodded.

"There was total chaos a minute ago and now everything is fine," said Lizzie. "Why hasn't anyone else noticed?"

"That's how the magic works," Mia said softly.

"Magic?" said Lizzie. "What magic?"

"Wish magic," Charlotte said.

"You can do magic?" asked Lizzie, sounding even more confused.

"We're training to become Secret Princesses," explained Mia. "We came here to grant your wish of making the Open Day a success."

"We've got three small wishes to help you," said Charlotte.

"Actually, only two now," Mia corrected. "We just used the first one."

"That's … incredible," said Lizzie.

"But you mustn't tell anyone," said Mia quickly, as Lizzie's parents approached them.

"Great news," said Lizzie's mum, beaming. "We've found a home for Jack and Jill."

"Amazing! Was it the family with two kids?" asked Lizzie.

Lizzie's dad nodded.

"Did anyone want to adopt Pickle?" Lizzie asked hopefully.

"I'm afraid not," said Lizzie's mum.

Lizzie sighed. "He's such a good dog," she said wistfully.

"Don't worry, sweetheart," said Lizzie's mum, patting her shoulder. "Pickle has a home here as long as he needs one."

"Speaking of Pickle," said Lizzie's dad, "I have to change his bandage. Do you want to come?"

"Yes please!" Lizzie said. "I need all the practice I can get if I'm going to be a vet

when I grow up," she told the girls. They all followed Lizzie's dad back inside. Pickle was curled up on a dog bed in his kennel, but he jumped up, his tail wagging, when he saw them.

Lizzie got Pickle out of his kennel. Charlotte and Mia stroked him and he wriggled happily. Lizzie's dad led them into the medical room, where there was an examining table and first-aid supplies. Placing Pickle on the table, Lizzie's dad gently unwrapped the bandage on his leg.

"Good boy," said Mia, stroking Pickle's head to keep him calm.

Lizzie's dad placed a clean gauze pad on the dog's wound and started wrapping a

fresh bandage around it.

"What are you doing?" someone asked. The little boy who'd bought the book was watching them from the doorway.

"Dad's giving the doggie a new bandage," explained Lizzie, passing her dad some tape to stick the bandage in place.

"Thanks, Lizzie. All done!" he said, peeling off his gloves.

"Can I pat him?" asked the boy shyly.

"He'd love that," said Lizzie, lifting Pickle down from the examining table. "His name is Pickle."

The sausage dog's tail thumped on the floor as the little boy stroked his back. "Hi, Pickle," the boy said. "I'm Ben."

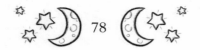

"Want to see how clever he is?" Lizzie asked.

Ben nodded, his eyes wide.

"Kiss," Lizzie told Pickle.

Pickle licked the little boy's cheek.

"Aw!" said Charlotte. "That's adorable."

"He likes me!" said Ben, giggling.

"He really does," said Lizzie, smiling as Pickle gave Ben another lick.

"There you are!" said Ben's mother, bursting into the medical room. "I've been looking everywhere for you!"

"I wanted to see the dogs," said Ben.

"It's time to do crafts," his mum said.

"Bye, Pickle," said Ben as his mum dragged him away.

"Oops!" Lizzie gasped. "I said I'd help Mum with the crafts!" Turning to Mia and Charlotte, she asked, "Are you any good at making things?"

"I'm hopeless," said Charlotte cheerfully. "But Mia loves doing crafts."

"Great," said Lizzie as she rushed off. "We're going to make cat toys. I'll meet you in the cat room!"

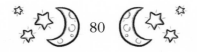

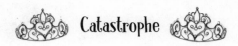

As Mia and Charlotte walked to the cattery, Charlotte said, "It's good that so many people turned up for the sanctuary Open Day."

"I just wish Hex had stayed away," said Mia. "And that horrible dog of his."

"We can handle them," said Charlotte confidently. "And I know what'll cheer you up – kittens!"

The cats lived in a warm, sunny room. They each had their own enclosure, with a little door leading to an outdoor run. Some cats were snoozing inside on comfy cushions, while others were sprawled in the sunshine outside.

A crowd of people were peering into an

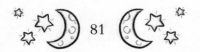

enclosure where a tabby mother cat was licking her kittens clean. One of the kittens was stripy like their mum and two were ginger. The tiniest one, which had ginger and white patches, let out a big yawn.

"Aww!" said Charlotte. "They're so adorable."

"They must be only a few days old," said Mia. "Their eyes are still shut."

In the middle of the room was a play area for the cats. There was a climbing frame that looked like a tree, its branches covered with carpet. Five cute black and white cats were playing in the enclosure.

"Hi!" said Lizzie as she and her mum came in holding a basket of craft supplies.

82

Mia and Charlotte helped Lizzie hand out sticks, ribbons and feathers.

"Cats love to play," said Lizzie. "So I'm going to show you how to make an easy cat toy." Lizzie tied a ribbon to the end of the stick, then she attached a feather to the other end of the ribbon. "You can take your toy home or leave it here," she said.

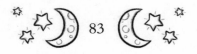

"We play with the cats every day so they don't get bored."

Mia and Charlotte walked around, helping the younger children.

"He likes it!" said a little girl with pigtails, dangling her toy for the little grey cat to swipe at.

"I'm going to make one of these for Flossie when I get home," Mia murmured to Charlotte.

"That's a nice kitty, isn't it?" said Ben's mum, as a sleek white cat batted the feather at the end of his toy.

Ben shrugged.

"Or how about this one?" said his mum, as a tortoiseshell cat purred and rubbed its

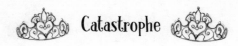

head against her legs.

"I want a dog," said Ben, pouting.

"Dogs are too big," said Ben's mum, stroking the tortoiseshell cat.

Suddenly, Ben's face lit up. "Look, Mummy!" he exclaimed. "A robot!"

Mia spun around and saw a small white robot with flashing green eyes wheel into the room. It was holding a cat basket.

"Cool!" cried the little girl with pigtails. The children clustered around the robot excitedly.

Mia and Charlotte exchanged looks. Unlike the other children, they weren't happy to see the robot – it was one of Princess Poison's helpers!

"What's the robot carrying?" asked the little girl.

"It must be a cat," said Lizzie, taking the basket from the robot. "Let's take a look."

"I don't think that's a good idea—" Charlotte warned.

Too late – Lizzie opened the basket. But there wasn't a cat inside ...

SQUEEAKKKKK!

Dozens of mice poured out of the cat basket! Squeaking and scurrying, they fled in every direction.

EEEEEEEEK!

Children and their parents shrieked and jumped out of the way. Ben's mum screamed as a mouse scurried over her foot!

YOWL!

The cats chased after the mice, baring their claws.

Mia watched in horror. If they didn't do something fast, the cats would eat the mice!

"We need to make another wish!" Mia cried out. Charlotte hurried over to her, tiptoeing to avoid the mice.

Holding her pendant next to Charlotte's, Mia said, "I wish for the mice to turn into something nice!"

CHAPTER SIX
Pigging Out!

Golden light lit up the cattery. A moment later, the real mice had transformed into colourful toy mice. Visitors who had been shrieking in fear a moment before were now laughing as they watched the cats play with their new toys.

The long-haired grey cat rolled around on the floor, holding the toy in its front paws.

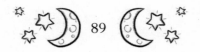

A tabby pounced on a toy mouse, grabbing it by the tail. The tortoiseshell miaowed happily as it chewed on a toy mouse's ear.

"They really like them," said Charlotte.

Mia picked up one of the toy mice and gave it a sniff. "They've got a herb called catnip in them," she said. "Cats love how it smells."

"Was that you guys again?" Lizzie whispered.

"We used another wish," Charlotte whispered back, winking.

"Where did that robot come from?" asked Lizzie. "I've never seen it before."

"It's called EVA," Mia told her. "It stands for Extra Villainous Assistant."

"It belongs to Princess Poison," explained Charlotte.

"Princess who?" asked Lizzie.

"Princess Poison," said Mia. "She's trying to spoil your wish. The robot and the man with the poodle both work for her."

"We still have one more wish left," Mia reassured Lizzie. "We're not going to let

Princess Poison – or any of her horrible helpers – spoil the Open Day."

The little girl with pigtails had picked up the grey cat and was cuddling it. The cat purred contentedly.

"Is this cat available to adopt?" asked the girl's mum.

"Smoky would love a new home," said Lizzie, looking thrilled.

"I can help with that!" Lizzie's mum said. As she took them off to do some paperwork, she called over her shoulder. "Lizzie, why don't you take everyone to see the small pets as well?"

"OK." Lizzie grinned. "If you want to meet rabbits, rats and guinea pigs, follow me!"

 92

Children and their parents followed Lizzie
out of the cattery.

Charlotte whispered to Mia, "Funny –
they didn't seem very keen on rodents a few
minutes ago!"

Mia grinned. Hopefully these ones
wouldn't be on the loose!

"Look what my dad and I made," Lizzie
said when they arrived.

She showed Mia and Charlotte a maze
with cardboard walls and soft shavings
on the ground. Two guinea pigs were
wandering around the maze, trying to get to
bowl of vegetables in the middle.

"That's so cool," said Mia.

"No, it's a-MAZING," said Charlotte.

"Who wants to hold a guinea pig?" asked Lizzie.

"Me!" cried all of the children.

"Can you help me?" Lizzie asked the girls.

"Of course," said Mia.

"You take Rosebud," said Lizzie, lifting a light brown guinea pig with a band of white around its belly out of the maze. She placed it in Mia's cupped hands.

"Hello, Rosebud," Mia said softly, caressing the little creature's soft back. Rosebud twitched her nose and stared at Mia with beady black eyes.

"This one is Freddie," said Lizzie, giving Charlotte a guinea pig with a mop of long black hair that flopped into his eyes.

Charlotte giggled. "He looks like a guinea pig rock star."

"Who wants to go first?" Lizzie asked.

A little girl wearing a princess outfit waved her hand wildly in the air. Lizzie gave her a towel to spread over her lap, then Mia gently placed Rosebud on it.

"This is Rosebud," said Mia. "What's your name?"

"Violet," said the little girl. "I mean, Princess Violet."

Mia smiled to herself. Maybe the little girl would be a princess one day – a Secret Princess, that is!

Charlotte put the long-haired guinea pig on Ben's lap. As Ben stroked Freddie, his mum snapped a photo of him with her phone.

"What a dear little thing," she said. "Maybe we should get a guinea pig – they're nice and small."

"But I want a dog, not a guinea pig," insisted Ben.

A tall, thin woman in a green dress and high heels opened the door. Her green eyes scanned the room, like a hawk looking for prey. Spotting Mia and Charlotte, her mouth twisted into a cruel smile.

"What fun!" Princess Poison said, tossing her black hair with its ice-white streak. She strode over and stroked Rosebud with a long-nailed finger. The guinea pig quivered, as if sensing danger.

"Thanks for coming to our Open Day," Lizzie said warmly.

"Are ALL animals
welcome at the
shelter?" Princess
Poison asked.

"Yes," said Lizzie.
"We never turn
animals away."

"Well, in that case
..." said Princess
Poison, pulling out
her wand.

With a wicked laugh, Princess Poison pointed it at the guinea pigs and said:

**"This shelter has enough
cats and dogs,
So turn these guinea pigs
into smelly hogs!"**

Green light shot from the wand and hit the guinea pigs, transforming them into huge pigs!

OINK! OINK! OINK!

The enormous pigs grunted loudly, snuffling around the room with their turned-up snouts. Their bristles were covered in mud and they smelled terrible.

"Pee-yew!" said the little girl in the princess dress. "Those piggies are really stinky."

Holding their noses, the visitors hurried out of the room to escape from the smell.

One of the hogs trampled over the guinea pigs' maze, crushing the cardboard walls and tunnels under its trotters.

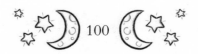

"My maze!" wailed Lizzie.

The other pig found a bag of rabbit food and ripped it open. Pellets spilled all over the floor and the pigs started gobbling them up, oinking happily.

"I'm afraid they're rather greedy hogs," said Princess Poison. "I hate to think how much it will cost to feed them."

"You're not going to spoil Lizzie's wish!" said Charlotte angrily.

"Hmm," said Princess Poison smugly, sauntering out of the room. "And pigs might fly!"

"Let me guess," said Lizzie. "That was Princess Poison."

"Yup," said Mia, sighing.

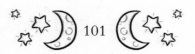

"I suppose we'll have to build them a pen outside," said Lizzie, staring at the pigs in dismay.

"You won't need to do that," said Charlotte. "I've got a better idea."

Charlotte and Mia held their necklaces together. The glow from their pendants was barely visible now, as there was only one wish left.

"I wish to change the pigs back into guinea pigs and fix the mess," said Charlotte.

With a flash of light, the hogs turned back into Rosebud and Freddie. The two little guinea pigs were inside a new maze – this one shaped like a castle with four turrets!

"Does it remind you of something?"
Charlotte asked Mia.

Mia grinned. The new maze did look a lot
like Wishing Star Palace! The smile faded
from her face as she remembered Princess
Luna, who was still waiting back at the
palace. If they didn't grant Lizzie's wish,
Luna would never get her magic back.

And the shelter's Open Day wasn't over – there was still the dog show ahead. If Princess Poison tried anything else, they didn't have any magic left to stop her!

CHAPTER SEVEN
The Cleverest Dog

"The dog show will start outside in five minutes!" Lizzie's mum's voice came over a loudspeaker.

"I'll meet you there," Lizzie told Mia and Charlotte. "I'm going to take Pickle. Maybe if someone sees him they'll adopt him!"

Outside, a crowd had gathered around a large roped-off area. Mia and Charlotte

squeezed in next to Ben and his mum, who were munching sandwiches.

"Thanks to all of you for coming," Lizzie's dad said into a microphone. "It's so lovely to see so many of our rescue dogs in their new happy homes."

All the dogs barked happily.

"The first prize today is for the waggiest tail," Lizzie's dad continued. "Anyone who wants to compete, step forward now!"

Several owners walked into the ring with their dogs.

SWISH! SWISH! SWISH! The dogs' tails wagged back and forth.

"What happy dogs," chuckled Lizzie's dad. He awarded the rosette to a fluffy chow

chow with a curly tail that was wagging so fast it was a blur.

"Hope I haven't missed much," said Lizzie, joining the girls with Pickle in her arms.

The next prize was for the dog most like its owner. A tall, thin man with a greyhound came forward.

"Oh, it's so good to see Betsy looking well," said Lizzie. "She was a racing dog but when she got injured and couldn't run, her old owner didn't want her any more."

"That's so mean," said Mia.

A deep growl startled Mia. She turned and saw a ferocious-looking dog with a spiky collar, straining on his lead.

"Good boy, Crusher," said Princess Poison.

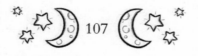

"Maybe you two should enter this category," said Charlotte. "That dog is as mean as you are."

"I'm not here to win the dog show." Princess Poison gave a horrible cackle. "I'm here to RUIN it!"

"But you've got pets," protested Lizzie. "Don't you want to help the shelter?"

"Don't be silly," scoffed Princess Poison.

"I only care about helping myself. And I'm going to do that by spoiling your wish."

Lizzie's dad awarded Betsy and her owner matching rosettes. "And now," he announced, "it's time for the fancy dress competition!"

Charlotte couldn't help giggling when she saw the dogs. There was a terrier in a ruffled collar and a clown hat, a plump bulldog in a superhero cape and a tiny chihuahua wearing fairy wings.

Hex hurried over to Princess Poison with his poodle. "Ooh! Look at them all! Can Miss Fluffy enter?" he asked. "You could make an amazing costume for her with your magic …"

Princess Poison scowled at her assistant. "No," she snapped. "Help me think of a curse to ruin this dog show."

"You could give all the dogs fleas," suggested Hex.

"Not bad," said Princess Poison. She drummed her long fingernails on her chin, thinking. "I've got it!" she said. "I'll cause a thunderstorm."

Hex chortled gleefully. "All dogs hate thunder. It will be a disaster!"

"EVA!" bellowed Princess Poison. "Come here now!"

The robot wheeled over obediently.

"Hold Crusher," Princess Poison ordered, giving the robot the dog's lead.

Princess Poison pointed her wand up at the sky.

> "Make lightning flash and thunder rumble,
> Then Lizzie's dreams will start to ..."

Before Princess Poison could finish her spell, Crusher lunged forward and tried to

bite Ben's sandwich. He tugged so hard
on his lead that EVA toppled over and
knocked the wand right out of Princess
Poison's hand.

GRRRRRR! Crusher snarled at Ben, his
sharp teeth bared. The vicious dog lunged
forward, ready to attack.

YAP! YAP! YAP! Pickle
wriggled out of Lizzie's
arms and jumped down.

He landed in front of Ben and stood his ground, barking to keep the bigger dog away.

Ben's mum heard the barking and quickly picked Ben up. At the same time Charlotte leapt forward and grabbed Crusher's lead.

"Ben!" cried the boy's mum, hugging him tight. "That little dog saved you!"

"His name is Pickle, Mummy," said Ben.

"What a brave boy!" Ben's mum praised Pickle.

Lizzie walked over to Crusher and told him to sit in a firm voice. Crusher looked a bit surprised, but then he plonked down on his bottom. "You're a good dog, really," Lizzie said. Crusher's tail wagged and he

rolled over on to his back, asking for a tummy tickle.

"There's no such thing as a bad dog, just a bad owner," Lizzie said.

"Crusher, get up!" Princess Poison shrieked. But Crusher was having too much fun. He rolled around on the floor until everyone was giggling.

Everyone except Princess Poison. She snatched his lead out of Charlotte's hands and stormed off, dragging Crusher away. Hex and EVA followed behind her.

Mia and Charlotte gave a sigh of relief as they left.

"Mummy, please can we take Pickle home with us?" Ben pleaded. "I love him. He's only little."

"Of course we can, darling," his mum said. "He's a hero." She crouched down to pat Pickle's head.

"Pickle – kiss!" Ben said.

The sausage dog gave Ben's mum a sloppy lick on her cheek.

"Oh my!" she said, laughing. "Too bad there isn't a category for cleverest dog. Pickle would win first prize!"

"He's found a new home," said Lizzie, beaming. "That's the best prize of all."

Ben's mum opened her handbag and took out her cheque book. "I'd like to make a donation to the shelter," she said, writing out a cheque.

Lizzie's mum's eyes widened in surprise as she saw the large amount Ben's mum had donated. "Thank you very much," she said. "That is very generous of you."

Lizzie's parents returned to the ring and

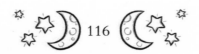

awarded the dog dressed as a clown first prize for best fancy dress costume. As Lizzie and her dad attached a rosette to the dog's collar, her mum announced, "Thank you all for coming. This has been the shelter's most successful Open Day ever!"

"We did it," said Mia, squeezing Charlotte's hand.

"Thank you so much," Lizzie said. She pinned a rosette on each of them. "You made my wish come true. You both deserve a prize for being amazing."

As Lizzie ran back to her parents, a soft voice behind the girls said, "Congratulations, girls." There was a flash of light and suddenly the rosettes magically

turned into huge flowers that burst and filled
the air with pretty petal confetti.

For a moment Mia didn't recognise
Princess Ella, who had on jeans and an
anorak instead of her princess dress. She
was carrying a big bag.

Ella went over to Ben, who was holding
Pickle. "I'm a vet," Ella said. "Is it OK if
I take a look at Pickle's leg?"

Ben nodded and handed Ella the sausage
dog. The girls followed Ella to a quiet spot
where she could examine Pickle.

"I'm so happy Pickle's found a home," Ella
said, unwrapping the dog's bandage.
She rummaged in her bag. Taking out her
wand, she touched it gently to Pickle's paw.

There was a flash of light and suddenly his wound was completely healed.

"Go to Ben," Ella told Pickle. Barking happily, Pickle ran back to Ben, his ears flapping in the breeze. He wasn't limping at all!

"Pickle!" Ben cried. "You're all better!"

Mia almost felt like crying as she watched Ben and Pickle playing together. They looked so happy!

"You didn't just grant Lizzie's wish today," said Ella. "You granted Ben's wish too." She touched her wand to Charlotte's necklace and a third moonstone appeared on the pendant. Then she gave Mia another moonstone, too.

"Princess Poison's curse on Luna is nearly broken," said Mia, gazing proudly at the three white stones embedded in her pendant.

"We just need to grant one more tiara star wish," said Charlotte.

"I'm sure you will," said Ella, smiling. "But right now it's time to go home. Why don't you say goodbye to your friend?"

"We've got to go," Charlotte told Lizzie when they found her.

Lizzie was in the middle of a load of dogs, rushing from one to another with a big smile on her face. When she spotted the girls she rushed over. "I'll never forget how you helped the shelter," she said, hugging

Mia and Charlotte. "We raised lots of money today – and even found a new home for Pickle!"

"I'm glad," said Mia, smiling. "This is an amazing place."

When they returned to Ella, Charlotte said, "Let's hope someone wishes on another tiara star soon!"

"Until then, send me some more cute animal videos," said Mia, hugging her friend goodbye.

"I will!" Charlotte laughed.

Ella waved her wand and the magic whisked the girls home.

A moment later, Mia was back in her kitchen, which smelled like chocolate. The brownies would soon be ready!

Mia snuggled up between Elsie and her mum on the sofa.

On the television screen, Alice was back in her pop star clothes. She turned to the camera and winked. "Tonight," she said, "the stars are shining even brighter than ever before."

Most people watching probably thought
she was talking about the performers,
but Mia knew what Alice really meant.
The stars were shining brighter than before
– because Mia and Charlotte had just
granted another tiara star wish!

The End

Join Charlotte and Mia in their
next Secret Princesses adventure

Read on for a sneak peek!

Movie Magic

"It's our turn now," said Charlotte Williams, rolling the dice. It was Sunday night and her family was playing a board game in their living room. Mum was on a team with Charlotte's twin little brothers but Charlotte and her dad were in the lead!

"Seven!" said her dad, moving their counter along to a green space.

"I'll read the question!" said Harvey,

taking a card from the box. "What do you call a group of meerkats?"

Dad and Charlotte looked at each other, their eyes the exact same shade of chocolate brown. Charlotte twiddled one of her brown curls as she tried to think of the answer.

"Any ideas?" Dad asked Charlotte hopefully.

Charlotte shook her head. "I wish Mia was here – she'd know the answer!"

Read Movie Magic to find out what happens next!

Homemade Cat Toys

Cats love to play! Here is an easy toy you can make for your favourite furry friend to play with.

eat Ball

u will need:
- 1 cardboard
- toilet paper roll
- scissors
- ruler
- pencil
- cat treat

Instructions:

1. Measure and mark four 1cm-wide rings on the side of the cardboard roll.

2. Cut out each ring with scissors.

3. Put the first ring into the second ring. Do the same with the third and the fourth, until you've made a ball.

4. Put a cat treat in the middle of the ball and watch your kitty have fun trying to get it out!

Secret
PRINCESSES

What would you wish for?

Are you a Secret Princess?

Join the Secret Princesses Club at:

secretprincessesbooks.co.uk

Explore the magic of the
Secret Princesses and discover:

❤ Special competitions! ❤
❤ Exclusive content! ❤
❤ All the latest princess news! ❤